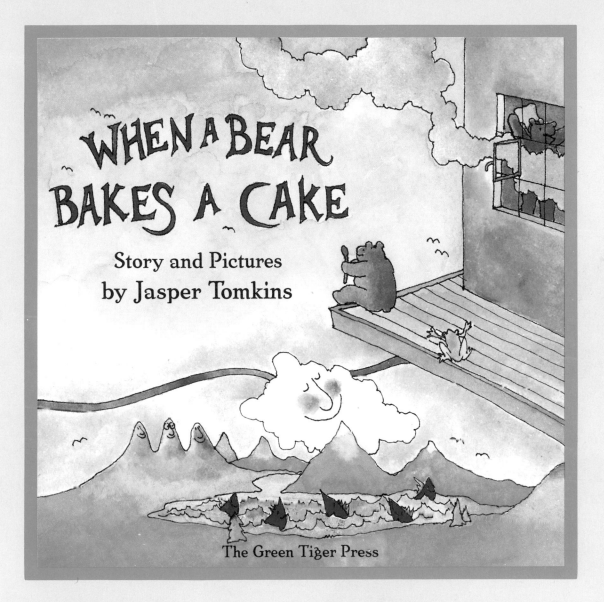

WHEN A BEAR BAKES A CAKE

Story and Pictures
by Jasper Tomkins

The Green Tiger Press

Story and Pictures copyright© 1987 by Jasper Tomkins
Green Tiger Press
First Edition
Library of Congress Card Catalog No. 87-80860
ISBN 0-88138-082-2
5 7 9 10 8 6
PRINTED IN HONG KONG

for the joy that thought bears

When a bear bakes a cake,
He throws it in the lake.

When a bear washes up,
He always breaks a cup.

When a bear sweeps the floor,
You can't get through the door.

When a bear takes a bath,
He rolls right down the path.

When a bear combs his hair,
He thinks that you're not there.

When a bear rides the train,
He hopes it doesn't rain.

When a bear comes for lunch,
He eats a great big bunch.

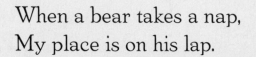

When a bear takes a nap,
My place is on his lap.

When a bear wants to hide,
He simply stands outside.

When a bear climbs a tree,
He's looking for the sea.

When a bear's out to sail,
You better start to bail.

When a bear's at the beach,
He makes a funny speech.

When a bear flies a kite,
He comes back late at night.

When a bear wears a pack,
His friend is on his back.

When a bear picks a flower,
He sits still for an hour.

When a bear finds some snow,
He puts on quite a show.

When a bear waits for fish,
He never gets his wish.

When a bear has a fire,
He swings by on a tire.

When a bear sings a song,
You hope it won't be long.

When a bear plays a fiddle,
There's dancing on the griddle.

When a bear gets the mail,
It comes up in a pail.

When a bear wears a suit,
He picks a lot of fruit.

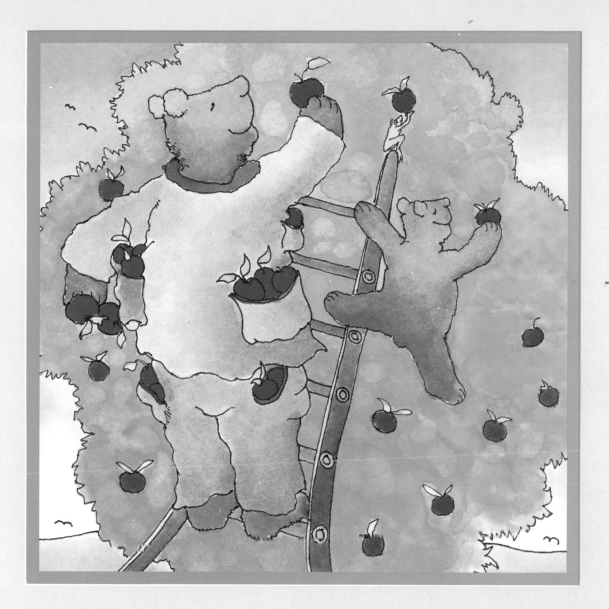

When a bear rides a bike,
He's really quite a sight.

When a bear stays up late,
He's sitting on the gate.

When a bear goes to bed,
You cannot see his head.

When a bear says goodnight,
It feels just right!